Stop the Grassfires!

by Patricia M. Stockland

illustrated by Ryan Haugen

visit us at
www.abdopublishing.com

Printed in the United States.

Text by Patricia M. Stockland
Illustrations by Ryan Haugen
Edited by Nadia Higgins
Interior layout and design by Becky Daum
Cover design by Becky Daum

Library of Congress Cataloging-in Publication Data
Stockland, Patricia M.
  Stop the grassfires! / Patricia M. Stockland ; illustrated by Ryan Haugen.
     p. cm. — (Safari friends—Milo & Eddie)
  ISBN 978-1-60270-086-4
 [1. Elephants—Fiction. 2. Monkeys—Fiction. 3. Rhinoceroses—Fiction. 4. Fires—Fiction. 5. Grasslands—Fiction. 6. Africa—Fiction.] I. Haugen, Ryan, 1972- ill. II. Title.
PZ7.S865Sto 2008
[E]—dc22

                    2007036993

"Yuck!" Milo the monkey wrinkled his nose. "What's that smell?"

"Oh, excuse me," replied Eddie the elephant, blushing.

"Not *that*," said Milo. "It smells like something is burning."

The pair peered across the savanna grasses. On the horizon, there was a rolling cloud of smoke and a faint glow of flames.

"Oh, dingoes! There is a fire! There is a *fire!*" exclaimed Eddie. "Hurry! We need to help!"

Milo hopped on Eddie's head, and the pair charged toward the smoke and flames. Alongside them, other worried animals galloped, trotted, swung, ran, and loped along the plain. Everyone wanted to stop the grassfires!

Milo and Eddie reached the smoky brush. The rest of Eddie's elephant herd was already there. Eloise and Ella were busily spraying down the smoldering grass with water from a nearby puddle.

But the elephants' efforts weren't enough. The fire was spreading across the great, great grassland, and the animals were starting to panic. The zebras couldn't stop zigzagging, and one worried lion broke out in tears.

"Eloise!" Eddie cried. "What can we do to help?"

Eloise turned around, sweat trickling down her trunk. "Well, don't just *stand* there! Make like peanuts and get cracking!"

Eddie didn't know quite what Eloise meant, but he understood the need for action.

"Milo!" Eddie said. "Let's get the rhinos!"

"The rhinos?" asked Milo, choking on smoke. "But the rhinos are snobs . . . unfriendly even. They might charge at us!"

"I think their terrible eyesight makes them seem unfriendly," replied Eddie. "I don't think they can see who's coming. So they charge at everyone. Let's just give them plenty of warning that we're coming, and I bet they'll help us."

Just then, Eloise bellowed at the pair, "Move it, already! We need to stop the grassfires!"

With that, Milo and Eddie were off again. They thundered down the trail at a full stomp and clomp.

"When we get closer, just start yelling the news. I'll do my part," Eddie instructed.

Milo was scared out of his monkey tail, but he did as he was told. From the somewhat safe top of Eddie's head, Milo started yelling, "HELP US! HELP US! WE NEED TO STOP THE GRASSFIRES!"

Then, across the grassland came a wild noise. . . .

"Cock-a-doodle woof woof meow!"

It was Eddie's trunk! Eddie was trumpeting his strange, not-so-useful trunk.

"Cock-a-doodle woof woof meow!"

And while it was a weird and wild noise, it definitely had the attention of the rhinos. At the sound of the strange ruckus, Rhett the rhino popped up his head from the grasses.

"What in the great, great grasslands is *that?*" he asked a nearby friend.

"Well, I can't see it, but it sounds an awful lot like an elephant whose trunk doesn't work."

"I can't see it either," answered Rhett, "but is that other sound a . . . monkey?"

"I do believe it is."

"Shh. Listen. I think they need help," said Rhett.

By now, Milo and Eddie were practically on top of the rhinos. They politely waited for the conversation to end before asking for help.

"Excuse us," said Eddie, "but the great, great grassland is on fire, and we need help! I hear you have superior hazard-proof, fire-stomping boots. We were hoping you could follow us and help stop the grassfires."

"I *do* declare!" exclaimed Rhett. "That's horrible news! Of course we'll help. Why didn't anyone ask sooner?"

"To be entirely honest," Eddie said, "the other animals are a bit scared of the constant charging."

"Oh, that . . . yes. Well, you see, we can't see that well. So, we charge at any noise, in case something dangerous sneaks up on us," explained Rhett.

Milo and Eddie smiled. "Yes, we see, we see," said Milo. "Now, um, about the fire. . . ."

"Heavens to hippos, yes! Let's get going!" cried Rhett. "We'll need you to lead the way, but we won't be able to see you very well. I don't suppose you'd be so kind as to trumpet?"

"But, of course!" Eddie exclaimed. And with that, he blew as hard as he could.

"Cock-a-doodle woof woof meow!"

The other animals soon heard the noise and felt the ground shake from the stomping and clomping. Milo, Eddie, Rhett, and a number of rumbling rhinos surrounded the fire.

The rhinos slipped on their special boots.

"Charge!" Rhett ordered. The rhinos galloped and stomped and stampeded and clomped. With each booming step, the smoke and flames fizzled. Soon the grassfires were stopped!

The animals cheered. The zebras kicked up their heels. The lion even stopped crying and hugged one of the hippos.

"Glad we could be of service," Rhett announced to the animals. And with that, the rhinos began rumbling back down the path toward home.

"But wait!" said Eddie. "What do we do if there's another fire? And shouldn't we thank you properly? And . . . and, well, wouldn't you like to stay and play?"

The rhinos stopped in their tracks.

"No one has ever asked us to play before," replied Rhett. The rhino grinned. "We would be delighted to."

The animals looked at each other. No one had ever played with a rhinoceros before. What did rhinos like to do? What were they good at?

"I have an idea!" Milo suddenly exclaimed. "How about a fire drill?"

Eloise piped up. "That is an *excellent* idea. In fact, the rhinos can be our official great grasslands firefighters. Rhett, would you be so kind as to lead us in a fire safety drill? That way, no one will gallop around in a panic or cry like a big kitten."

"I absolutely agree," said Rhett. "And we would love to lead the fire safety drill. We'll just need someone to get us a good fire alarm. We would have a hard time seeing the smoke. . . ."

"Don't worry," said Eddie. "I can announce a fire! Cock-a-doodle woof woof meow!"

Milo giggled. Then the lion started laughing, and soon the hyenas were in hysterics.

Eddie just shrugged and smiled. "Glad to be of service!" he said. "Cock-a-doodle woof woof meow!"

Savanna Facts

Black rhinos are endangered, which means the species could die off completely.

Rhinos are nearsighted. They have a difficult time seeing things far away. So, they often charge at things when they are surprised or startled.

Lightning can start grassfires on the savanna. Sometimes, researchers burn small parts of the savanna during the wet season. These controlled fires help burn off extra weeds and grasses. This way, if a fire starts during the dry season, it doesn't have as much fuel.